FIND IT! CHRISTMAS

A BIG BOOK OF SEARCH & FIND ADVENTURES

Have fun completing the search-and-find activities in this book!

At the back of the book, there are card press-outs for you to decorate and display or give away.

There are also over 500 stickers to decorate your press-outs or use wherever you want!

make believe ideas

TRIM THE TREE

The ORNAMENTS glitter
as BRIGHT as can be,
ready to HANG on the beautiful TREE!

LOOK up and down and try to find
which decoration is ONE OF A KIND?

 Who's ASLEEP?

Who has a SOCK?

 Who has curly ANTLERS

Who's wearing a BOW TIE?   Who has lost a CROWN?

FLYING ANGELS

The beautiful **ANGELS** are ready to **FLY** — they're flapping their **WINGS** in the bright morning **SKY!**

LOOK up and down and try to find which flying creature is **ONE OF A KIND?**

Who has a **WAND?** Which halo is **HEART SHAPED?** Who looks **SAD?**

Who hasn't got WINGS? ⟳ Who's UPSIDE DOWN? ⟳ Who has lost his HALO?

CHRISTMAS CARDS

The colorful **CARDS** are written with cheer:
"MERRY CHRISTMAS to you,
and a happy **NEW YEAR!**"

LOOK up and down and try to find
which sweet card is **ONE OF A KIND?**

What has lost its STAR?   Who's SLEEPING?   Who has lost a HAT?

What's UPSIDE DOWN?　∿　Which CANDLE is unlit?　∿　Where is the KITTEN?

KITTY CAROLS

The **KITTENS** like to spread good CHEER
by singing sweet **CAROLS**
for people to HEAR!

LOOK up and down and try to find
which squeaky creature is **ONE OF A KIND?**

Who's holding a WALKING STICK?   Who's playing a TRUMPET?

Who's standing on a TAMBOURINE?   Who's facing the WRONG way?

DELIGHTFUL DEER

The REINDEER are in the WOODS today, preparing to pull SANTA'S PRESENT-FILLED sleigh!

LOOK up and down and try to find which grizzly animal is ONE OF A KIND?

Who's dressed as SANTA? Who has LIGHTS in his antlers? Who has a STAR

Whose antlers are TREES?   Who has ORNAMENTS in her antlers?

SANTA'S LITTLE HELPERS

The **ELVES** in the workshop are making TOYS
so that SANTA can give them
to good **GIRLS** and **BOYS!**

LOOK up and down and try to find
which flying helper is **ONE OF A KIND?**

Who has a striped **CANDY CANE?**   Who's wearing **ANTENNAE?**

Who has a MUSTACHE? ᶜᵘ Who has a GIFT? ᶜᵘ Who has two STOCKINGS?

PLAYFUL PENGUINS

The **PENGUINS** are playing out in the SNOW,
with **SLEDS** and **SKATEBOARDS**
and SNOWBALLS to throw!

LOOK up and down and try to find
which black-and-white animal is **ONE OF A KIND?**

Who has FALLEN? ~ Where is the ROBIN? ~ Who has lost his EARMUFFS?

Who wears a BEAR HAT? ⟳ Who's on a SKATEBOARD? ⟳ Who has a BABY?

SURPRISE
PRESENTS

The pretty **PRESENTS** are WRAPPED and tied.
What tempting **TREATS** could be HIDDEN inside?

LOOK up and down and try to find
which roaring present is **ONE OF A KIND?**

Who has lost a RIBBON? ~ Where are the ICE SKATES? ~ Who's ASLEEP?

What has turned STRIPY?   Where is the BUS?   What's on its SIDE?

SECRET SANTAS

SANTA is busy and RUSHED off his feet,

so make sure to leave him

some COOKIES to eat!

LOOK up and down and try to find

which festive lady is ONE OF A KIND?

Who's ICE SKATING? ~ Who has a COOKIE? ~ Who has a PRESENT?

Who has a festive SWEATER?   Who has lost his GLASSES?

LET IT SNOW

The SNOWMEN chill in the WINTER sun,
throwing their SNOWBALLS
and having such FUN!

LOOK up and down and try to find
which purring animal is ONE OF A KIND?

Who has lost a TASSEL?   Who's wearing EARMUFFS?   Who is SAD?

Who has GLASSES? ～ Who has lost his NOSE? ～ Who's MELTED? ～

STOCKING FILLERS

The **STOCKINGS** brim with wonderful TREATS.
There are new **TOYS** to play with
and candies so SWEET!

LOOK up and down and try to find
which piece of clothing is **ONE OF A KIND?**

Which GINGERBREAD MAN is alone? Who's UPSIDE DOWN?

Where is the TOY TRAIN? Which stocking is EMPTY?

WARM AND SNUG

The cuddly POLAR BEARS huddle together to keep themselves WARM in the COLD, snowy weather.

LOOK up and down and try to find which feathery creature is ONE OF A KIND?

Who's wearing a CARDIGAN? Who has SUNGLASSES?

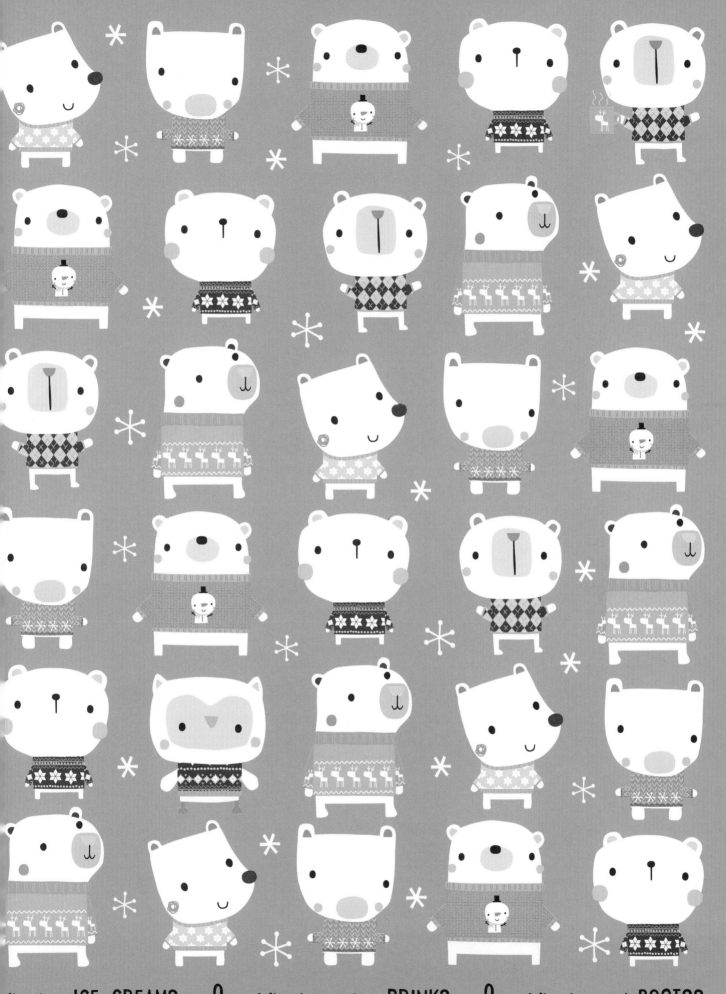

Who has ICE CREAM? ᴄⳑ Who has a hot DRINK? ᴄⳑ Who has red BOOTS?

SWEET TREATS

When **CHRISTMAS** comes, it's fun to eat sweet gingerbread HOUSES and **CANDY-CANE** treats!

LOOK up and down and try to find which zooming treat is **ONE OF A KIND?**

What has lost a STAR? What has lost its STRIPES?

Who has lost a HAT? ∿ Who has a PONYTAIL? ∿ What has lost a CHIMNEY?

TWINKLING TREES

The **TREES** are dressed up in glittering LIGHTS, with **TWINKLING** branches that GLOW through the night!

LOOK up and down and try to find which little fruit tree is **ONE OF A KIND?**

Which tree has lost a **FAIRY**?   Which tree is in a **BOOT**?

hich tree has a BOW? ∿ Which tree is BARE? ∿ Which candles are OUT?

FOREST
FRIENDS

The ANIMALS happily play as it SNOWS.
Their magical PLAYGROUND
GLITTERS and glows!

LOOK up and down and try to find
which jungle animal is ONE OF A KIND?

Which tree has PRESENTS? ～ Who's wearing a HAT? ～ Who's SLEDDING

ho has found a BIRD? ∽ Who has a PRESENT? ∽ Who has lost her SCARF?

On the next pages, there are fun press-outs for you to decorate and display or give away.

Here's how to use your press-out pieces:

1 Pull out the card pages at the back of the book.

2 Gently push the shapes until they pop out.

3 Complete the press-out pieces using pens and your stickers.

How to make your press-out angels and fairy:

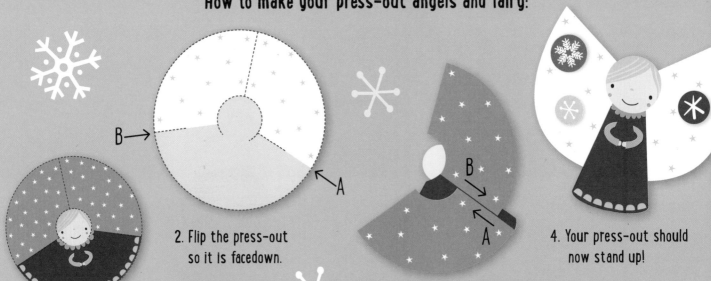

1. Press out the character.

B→

2. Flip the press-out so it is facedown.

A

3. Cross the wings to slide wing A into wing B.

B

A

4. Your press-out should now stand up!

Cards and Gift Tags

To:

From:

To:

From:

To:

From:

To:

From:

To:

From:

To:

From:

To:

From:

Festive Decorations

Stickers for cards and gift tags

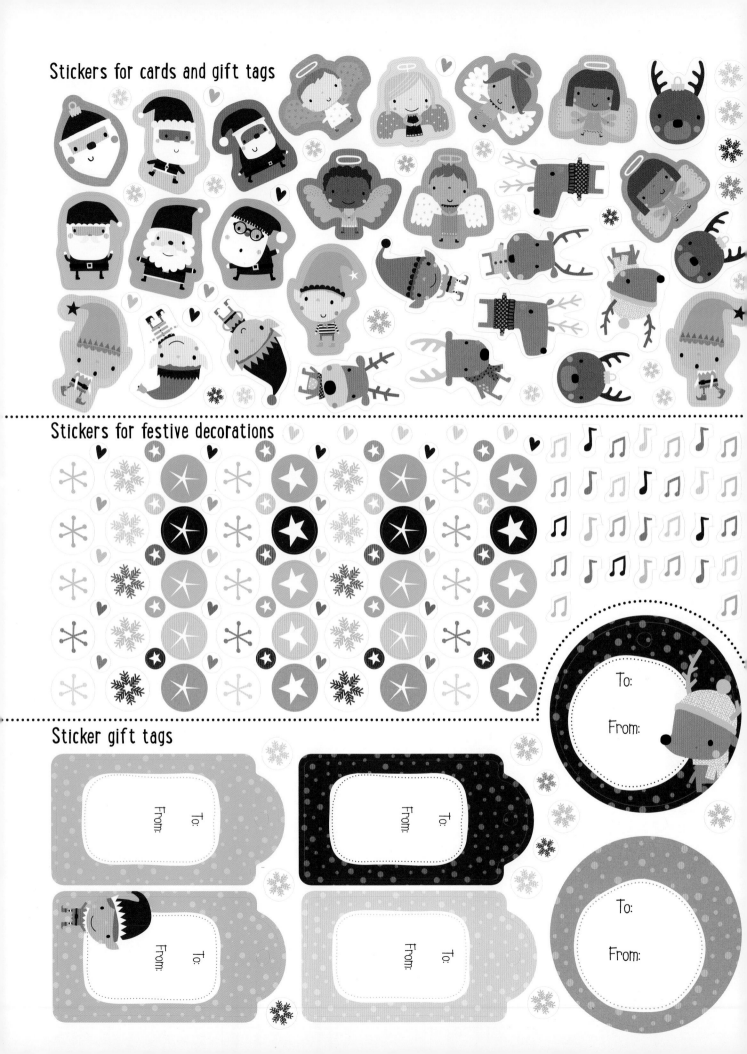

Stickers for festive decorations

Sticker gift tags

To:

From:

From: To:

From: To:

From: To:

To:

From:

Extra stickers